W9-CMI-815

Dear Parent:

Congratulations! Your child is taking the first steps on an exciting journey. The destination? Independent reading!

STEP INTO READING® will help your child get there. The program offers five steps to reading success. Each step includes fun stories and colorful art. There are also Step into Reading Sticker Books, Step into Reading Math Readers, Step into Reading Phonics Readers, Step into Reading Write-In Readers, and Step into Reading Phonics Boxed Sets—a complete literacy program with something to interest every child.

Learning to Read, Step by Step!

Ready to Read   Preschool–Kindergarten
• big type and easy words • rhyme and rhythm • picture clues
For children who know the alphabet and are eager to begin reading.

Reading with Help   Preschool–Grade 1
• basic vocabulary • short sentences • simple stories
For children who recognize familiar words and sound out new words with help.

Reading on Your Own   Grades 1–3
• engaging characters • easy-to-follow plots • popular topics
For children who are ready to read on their own.

Reading Paragraphs   Grades 2–3
• challenging vocabulary • short paragraphs • exciting stories
For newly independent readers who read simple sentences with confidence.

Ready for Chapters   Grades 2–4
• chapters • longer paragraphs • full-color art
For children who want to take the plunge into chapter books but still like colorful pictures.

STEP INTO READING® is designed to give every child a successful reading experience. The grade levels are only guides. Children can progress through the steps at their own speed, developing confidence in their reading, no matter what their grade.

Remember, a lifetime love of reading starts with a single step!

For Ramona, Leo, and Anthony,
who always share their jelly beans.
—A.J.

Visit us on the Web!
StepIntoReading.com
randomhouse.com/kids

Educators and librarians, for a variety of teaching tools, visit us at
randomhouse.com/teachers

ISBN: 978-0-7364-2857-6 (trade)—ISBN: 978-0-7364-8097-0 (lib. bdg.)
Printed in the United States of America   10 9 8 7 6 5 4 3 2 1

STEP INTO READING®  STEP 1

The Bunny Surprise

By Apple Jordan

Illustrated by Mario Cortés
and the Disney Storybook Artists

Random House 🏠 New York

It is Easter morning.

Bonnie finds
an Easter basket!

The basket is full
of surprises.

Candy, eggs,
and jelly beans!

The toys see a bunny
in the basket.

They think
it is a new toy.

Woody says howdy.

The bunny
does not say hello.

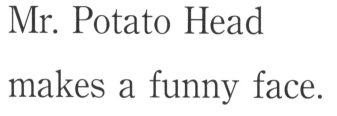

Mr. Potato Head

makes a funny face.

The bunny
does not giggle.

Mr. Pricklepants

sings and dances.

The bunny
does not clap or cheer.

Rex and Trixie

play a game.

The bunny

does not play along.

Dolly has a tea party.

The bunny
does not sip tea.

Is the bunny sleeping?
Buzz sounds his laser.

The bunny does not
wake up.

Why doesn't the bunny
want to play?

Here comes Bonnie!
Will she play
with the bunny?

Bonnie bites
the bunny's ear!

The toys are shocked!

Then they see.

The bunny

is not a toy . . .

29

. . . it is
a <u>chocolate</u> bunny!

Everyone laughs.

This Easter is full
of surprises!